For Sue

First published in hardback in Great Britain by HarperCollins Children's Books in 2010
First published in paperback in 2011

3 5 7 9 10 8 6 4 2

ISBN: 978-0-00-726385-1

HarperCollins Children's Books is a division of HarperCollins Publishers Ltd.

Text and illustrations copyright © Oliver Jeffers 2010

Visit our website at www.harpercollins.co.uk

Printed in China

Up and Down

This
WAY →

OLIVER JEFFERS

HarperCollins *Children's Books*

Once there were two friends...

and they always did
everything together.

Until one day the penguin decided there was something important he wanted to do all by himself...

He did own wings after all,

even if they didn't work very well.

Although that didn't stop
the penguin from trying.

And trying.

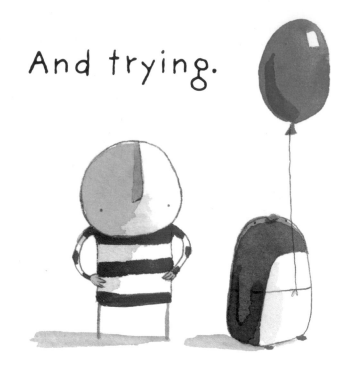

But nothing worked,
and it wasn't long before
he ran out of ideas.

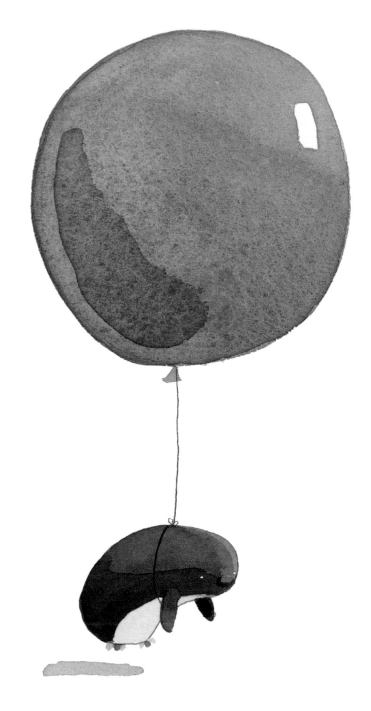

The boy even offered him a go
in his plane, but the engine hadn't
recovered from its last flight.

And besides, it wasn't the same.
The penguin wanted to do this by himself.

After doing a bit of homework,
it seemed as though the odds were
against him.

So together the boy and the penguin
decided it was time to ask for help...

EVER DREAMED of FLYING?

ARE YOU SHORT & FAT?

The TRAVELLING SHOW IS LOOKING FOR A NEW LIVING ☆ CANNONBALL

when something caught the penguin's eye and he knew this was his chance.

OWLS →

NARWHA →

In his
excitement,
he rushed off
without a word.

The boy didn't know
where he had gone.

The boy looked everywhere,
and even thought he'd
found his friend
for a second.

Although none
of these other penguins
knew how to play his favourite game.

Meanwhile, the penguin had found the right place and was hired on the spot.

Soon he'd get to fly...

but suddenly, he realised
he didn't know where
his friend was or how
to get home.

Later that night,
the penguin couldn't
help but miss
his friend.

Likewise, the boy could barely sleep for worrying about *his* friend.

The next day, the boy tried to think
of all the places the penguin would go,

ALL NEW

LIVING
CANNON BALL
TONIGHT!

GATE
4

when something caught his eye.
He didn't have much time.

The penguin's big moment had come but somehow
he wasn't so sure about flying anymore.

He wished the boy were there and even
wondered if his friend had noticed he'd gone?

But it was too late for thoughts like that.

BAM!

He took off like a bullet!

The boy rushed in hoping he could still catch his friend.

He was terrified and wished
his friend was there to help him.

The boy was there to catch him.

The friends agreed that there was
a reason why his wings didn't
work very well...

because penguins don't like flying.

So together
the two friends
made a break
for home...

to play their favourite game.